THE DEAD MAN

Georges Bataille

TRANSLATED BY
Jayne Austen

ILLUSTRATIONS BY
Andy Masson

INTRODUCTION BY
Lord Ouch

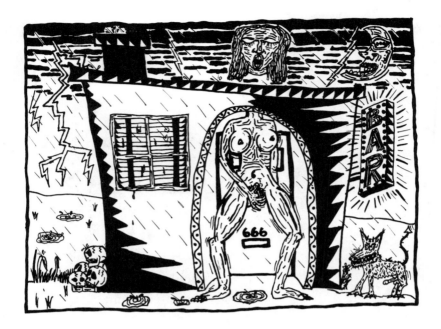

This edition printed by permission of Marion Boyars Publishers New
York, London. A translation of THE DEAD MAN by Austryn Wainhouse
appeared originally in MY MOTHER, MADAME EDWARDA and THE
DEAD MAN in one volume, published by Marion Boyars Publishers.

Ediciones La Calavera • P.O. Box 1106 Peter Stuyvesant Station
New York, New York 10009

MARIE'S SOVEREIGNTY

By Lord Ouch

"All it takes is to imagine suddenly the charming little girl whose soul would be Dali's abominable mirror..." If I had to imagine Bataille's "charming little girl" she would be the blonde, demonic child that appears at the end of Fellini's short film *Toby Dammit.* An incarnation of Satan holding a large red ball which is really Toby's head lost in a wager. She would bear the names: Simone, Marcelle, Lazare, Dirty, Eponine, and of course Marie.

How does one explain Bataille's body of work, which like all bodies, physical and metaphorical, is assumed to be unified and containing on the one hand the jerking off of an encephalitic dwarf, and on the other a critique of the Marshall Plan.

Perhaps it is necessary to reconstruct the image of the "body" of the work. To sever the Cartesian head that thinks with a "clear and assured consciousness of that which is useful in life." No longer a seamless whole, a series of discourses revealing a full positivity but something like the image of the Acephale; headless, sacred heart in its right

hand, dagger in its left, self-mutilating, a labyrinth of en-
trails, the skull of genitals. The bowels are a labyrinth where
food finds its soul to be shit. The night is a labyrinth where
Marie...

What gender is Bataille's excess? What sex?

About the *Story of the Eye* Barthes says "the erotic theme...is
never directly phallic." Or as Leiris writes concerning the
novel's erotic activity; "innumerable possible permutations
in a universe so little hierarchized that all is interchangeable
there." Bataille replaces the strictures of gender, sexuality
and hierarchy, with the orgy of metaphoric chains and their
inexorable combinations; eye/egg/testicle.

For example, Simone's vagina transforms from the sex
organ which Marcelle and the narrator adore, to the mouth
that devours the bull's testicle, and then to the socket for the
priest's eye that is the sad gaze of Marcelle. Vagina/mouth/
eye socket. All of the elements of the story go through these
changes, experience the random mutations of the basic
metaphor. Always in threes, like a perverse parody of the
Holy Trinity. The Father, the Son and the Holy Ghost. The
Eye, the Egg and the Holy Testicle. The hierarchy of gender,
the dominance of the phallus broken by metaphor, by a new
and obscene grammar.

The Deadman raises the question "What gender is
Bataille's concept of sovereignty?" But gender is a poor
word when speaking of sovereignty. Gender is a social con-
struction, a figure created by the work of discourse.

It is the story of Marie's escape and transgression initi-
ated by Edward's death, by his sacrifice. It is the sacrifice of
Edward that opens the possibility of the sacred. "The victim

dies, thus the witnesses participate in an element which his death reveals. This element is what it is possible for us, along with religious historians, to call the *sacred*. The sacred is precisely the continuity of being revealed to those who fix their attention, in a solemn rite, on the death of a discontinuous being." *The Deadman* is Marie's night of sovereignty, her "practice of joy before death." Her useful and everyday world crumbles away, replaced by a life rushing headlong towards death and silence. Along the way towards death preparations with drunkeness, debauchery, and the "little death" of orgasm. Burning with the *"la part maudite,"* the excremental, and the heterogeneous, Marie recaptures a life which has been forgotten, repressed by a limited economy of accumulation, equivalence and project. The memory of this sovereignty would be something like the memory involved in the phantom limb of an amputee.

In *The Deadman* Bataille mixes mortality and dark burlesque; the death rattle, orgasm and wail of laughter which combine to create a total abjection. Thus it is a sacred text. It is also a Hegelian text. Or rather a text that wrestles with Hegel's imperial system. If Marie is the character of sovereignty then the Count embodies Hegel's concept of *Herrschaft*. A laughable, deformed figure that deserves our respect and derision, much like Hegel's system.

Brooklyn, 1989

WHEN Edward fell back dead, a void opened in her, a long shudder ran down her, which lifted her up like an angel. Her naked breasts stood up in an imaginary church where the feeling of the irretrievable emptied her. Standing, near the dead man, absent, outside herself, in a slow ecstasy, overwhelmed. She knew she was in despair, but she played with her despair. Edward, as he died, had begged her to strip herself naked.

She hadn't been able to do it in time! She was there, in disarray: only her breasts jutted out of the ripped dress.

MARIE REMAINS ALONE
WITH THE DEAD EDWARD

T H E time had come to deny the laws to which fear subjects us. She pulled off her dress and put her coat on her arm. She was crazy and naked. She rushed outside and ran into the night in the downpour. Her shoes smacked in the mud and the rain eddied down her. She had to go very badly, but she held it in. In the softness of the woods, Marie stretched out on the ground. She pissed for a long time, urine drenched her legs. On the ground she sang in a crazy impossible voice:

> . . . there is some nudity
> and some atrocity . . .

Then she got up, put her raincoat back on and ran through Quilly up to the door of the inn.

MARIE GOES OUT
OF THE HOUSE NAKED

D A Z E D, she remained in front of the door, lacking the courage to go in. She heard coming from inside, screams, the songs of whores and drunks. She felt herself trembling, but she took pleasure in this trembling.

She thought, "I'll go in, they'll see me naked." She had to lean against the wall. She opened her coat and put her long fingers in her slit. She listened, fixed with anxiety, she breathed in the smell of her ill-washed sex. In the inn, they were screeching away, then everything went silent. It was raining: in a cellarlike darkness, a warmish wind slanted the rain. The voice of a whore sang a sad song about the working class districts on the edge of town. Heard outside, in the night, the dark voice veiled by the walls was excruciating. It went silent. Applause and the stamping of feet followed, then clapping in rhythm.

Marie was sobbing in the darkness. She cried in her helplessness, the back of her hand against her teeth.

MARIE WAITS
IN FRONT OF THE INN

K N O W I N G that she would be going in, Marie trembled. She opened the door, took three steps into the room: a gust of wind closed the door behind her.

She remembered having imagined this door forever slammed upon her.

The farmboys, the woman who kept the bar and the whores all stared at her.

She stood motionless at the entrance; muddy, hair streaming with water, and just generally looking bad. She looked as if she had floated up on the squall of the night (you could hear the wind outside). Her coat covered her, but she pulled back the collar.

MARIE GOES INTO
THE INN

S H E asked in a quiet voice:

—Got anything to drink?

The barkeeper answered from behind the bar:

—Calva?

She poured a shot at the bar.

Marie wouldn't take it.

—I want a bottle and some glasses she said.

Her quiet voice was firm.

She added:

—I'm drinking with them.

She paid.

One of the farmboys with dirt on his boots said timidly:

—You just dropped in for some entertainment?

—That's right, said Marie.

She tried to smile: the smile bored right through her.

She took a seat by the boy, rubbed her leg up against his, took his hand and placed it between her thighs.

When the boy touched the slit, he moaned:

—In the Name of God!

Excited, the others kept quiet.

One of the girls, getting up, lifted up one of her coattails.

—Take a look at this, she said, she's naked as the day she was born.

Marie let her go on and emptied a glass of liquor.

—She's used to milk, said the woman behind the bar.

Marie belched bitterly.

MARIE DRINKS
WITH THE FARMBOYS

M A R I E said sadly:

—That's a fact.

Her wet black curls stuck to her face in ringlets. She shook her pretty head, got up, took off her coat.

A lout who had been drinking in the inn moved toward her. He staggered, beating the air with his arms. He screeched out:

—All naked ladies up for grabs!

The woman behind the bar warned him:

—I'll twist your ugly beak . . .

She grabbed his nose and twisted it.

He screeched.

—No, try there, said Marie, it works better.

She walked up to the drunk and unbuttoned his fly: she pulled out of his trousers his half-limp dick.

The dick raised a great burst of laughter.

In one gulp, Marie, bold as a beast, sucked down a second glass.

The barkeeper, eyes like searchlights, gently touched her behind near the cleft.

—Good enough to eat, she said.

Marie filled her glass again. The liquor gurgled out.

She slugged it down like she was dying. The glass fell from her hands. Her behind was flat and nicely cleft. Her softness lit up the room.

M A R I E   P U L L S   O U T   T H E
D I C K   O F   A   D R U N K A R D

O N E of the farmboys was standing over in the corner with a hateful look on his face. He was just a little too good-looking a man, in high crepe rubber boots, that were just a little too new.

Marie came up to him with the bottle in her hand. She was feeling good and she was excited. Her legs swayed in her floating stockings. The boy took the bottle and took a slug. He screamed out in a fierce, unthinkable voice:

—Enough!

Slamming the empty bottle straight down on the table. Marie asked him:

—Want another?

He answered with a smile: he was treating her like a conquest.

He started up the player piano. He pretended, when he came back, to dance a little dance with his arms curved out in front of him.

He took Marie by the hand, they danced an obscene java. Marie gave herself up to it completely, nauseated, her head thrown back.

M A R I E   D A N C E S
W I T H   P I E R R O T

T H E barkeeper all of a sudden jumped up screaming:
   —Pierrot!
Marie was falling: she escaped from the arms of the beautiful
boy who tripped.
The thin body, which had been gliding along, fell to the floor
with the noise of a beast.
   —The little whore! said Pierrot.
He wiped his mouth with the back of his sleeve.
The barkeeper rushed over. She knelt down and raised her
head with care: saliva, or rather drool was running from her
lips.
One girl brought over a moistened towel.
In a short time, Marie came to. She asked weakly:
   —Liquor!
   —Give her a glass, said the barkeeper to one of the girls.
They gave her a glass. She drank and said:
   — More!
The girl filled her glass. Marie lifted it out of her hands. She
drank as if she was running out of time.
Nestling in the arms of one of the girls and the barkeeper,
she lifted her head:
   —More! she said.

MARIE FALLS DOWN
DEAD DRUNK

T H E farmboys, the girls and the barkeeper surrounded
Marie waiting to see what she was going to say.
Marie murmured only one word:

    — . . . the dawn, she said.

Then her head fell back heavily. Sick, very sick . . .
The barkeeper asked:

    —What'd she say?

No one knew what to answer.

MARIE TRIES
TO SPEAK

T H E N the barkeeper said to pretty Pierrot:

—Suck her.

—Should we put her on a chair? said one girl.

Several of them grabbed her body at once and managed to get her ass onto the chair.

Pierrot, kneeling down, slipped her legs over his shoulders. The young stud had a smile of conquest and darted his tongue into her crotch hair.

Sick, lit-up, Marie seemed happy, she smiled without opening her eyes.

M A R I E   I S   S U C K E D
B Y   P I E R R O T

S H E felt lit-up, frozen over, but endlessly emptying, emptying her life into the sewer.

A helpless desire maintained a tension in her: she would
have liked to let that tension in her belly go. She imagined
the horror of the others. She was no longer separated from
Edward.

Her cunt and her ass naked: the smell of her ass and her wet
cunt freed her heart and the tongue of Pierrot, that wet her,
seemed like the coldness of death to her.

Drunk with liquor and with tears and not crying, she drank
in this cold, her mouth open: she pulled over to her the head
of the barkeeper, opening to the woman's decaying teeth
the voluptuous abyss of her lips.

MARIE KISSES
THE BARKEEPER
ON THE MOUTH

MARIE pushed the woman away and she saw her head, hair dishevelled, twisted out of itself with joy. The face of the virago radiated drunken tenderness. She was drunk too, sentimental drunk: devoted tears came to her eyes.

Looking at these tears and seeing nothing, Marie was living bathed in the light of the dead man. She said:

—I'm thirsty.

Pierrot was sucking hard enough to take his breath away.

Hurriedly, the barkeeper gave her a bottle.

Marie drank in long gulps and emptied it.

MARIE DRINKS
IN HUGE GULPS

. . . S C U F F L I N G, a cry of terror, a confusion of broken bottles, Marie's thighs twitched like a frog's. The boys were screaming and shoving for position. The barkeeper helped Marie, laid her out on the bench.

Her eyes remained empty, ecstatic.

The wind, the squall, outside, were going crazy. In the night, the shutters banged away.

—Listen, said the barkeeper.

They heard the howling of the wind in the trees, long and moaning like the cry of a mad woman.

The door at that moment was wide open, a gust of wind blew into the room.

Instantly, naked Marie found herself standing up.

She cried out:

—*Edward!*

And the anguish made her voice a prolonging of the wind.

MARIE COMES

F R O M this bad night , came a man, struggling to close an umbrella: his rat-like silhouette stood out in the doorway.

—Quickly, your lordship! come in, said the barkeeper. She staggered.

The dwarf came forward without answering.

—You're soaked, the woman continued, closing the door.

The little man was possessed of a surprising gravity, enormous and hunchbacked, with a huge head crowning his shoulders. He greeted Marie, then turned towards the farmboys.

—Good day, Pierrot, he said shaking his hand, take my coat if you would.

Pierrot helped the count to remove his overcoat. The count gave him a pinch on the thigh.

Pierrot smiled. The count shook people's hands amicably.

—May, I? he asked as he bowed.

He took a seat at Marie's table across from her.

—A few bottles, would you, said the count.

—I've drunk, said one girl, so much I could piss on my chair.

—Drink enough to shit, my child . . .

He stopped crisply, rubbing his hands.

Not without a certain detachment.

MARIE ENCOUNTERS
A DWARF

MARIE remained motionless looking at the count and his head turned toward her.

—Pour, she said.

The count filled the glasses.

She said again, very wisely:

—I'm going to die at dawn. . .

The count's steely look moved up and down her.

His blond eyebrows went up, accentuating the wrinkles in his excessively wide forehead.

Marie lifted her glass and said:

—Drink!

The count also lifted his glass and drank: they greedily emptied their glasses in unison.

The barkeeper came and sat down near Marie.

—I'm afraid, Marie said to her.

Her eyes never left the count.

She made a kind of coughing: she murmured in a crazed voice into the ear of the old woman:

—It's the ghost of Edward.

—Edward? asked the woman quietly.

—He's dead, said Marie in the same voice.

She took the other woman's hand and bit it.

—You bitch, screamed the woman who'd been bitten.

But freeing her hand, she caressed Marie and kissing her on the shoulder, she said to the count:

—All the same, she's sweet.

MARIE SEES
THE GHOST OF EDWARD

T H E count in his turn asked:

—Who is Edward?

—You no longer know who you are, said Marie.

This time her voice broke:

—Make him drink, she demanded of the barkeeper.

She seemed to be at the end of her rope.

The count snorted down his glass but admitted:

—Liquor has very little effect on me.

The enormous little man with the excessively large head scanned Marie with a mournful eye, as if he had had the intention of annoying her.

He scanned everything in the same way, his head stiff between his shoulders.

He called out:

—Pierrot!

The boy approached:

—This young child, said the dwarf, has given me a hard-on. How about sitting yourself down here?

When the farmboy was seated, the count added gaily:

—Be nice, Pierrot, jerk me off. I don't dare ask this child . . .

He smiled.

—She isn't accustomed, as you are, to monsters.

At that moment, Marie got up on top of the bench.

MARIE GETS UP
ON TOP OF
THE BENCH

—I'M afraid, said Marie. You look like a fence post.
He didn't answer. Pierrot grabbed his prick.
He was in fact impassive as a fence post.
—Go away, Marie told him, or I'll piss on you . . .
She got up on the table and squatted down.
—I'd be only too delighted, responded the monster. His neck had no freedom of movement: if he spoke, his chin alone moved.
Marie pissed.
Pierrot vigorously jerked off the count who was struck in the face with urine.
The count turned red and urine drenched him. Pierrot was jerking him off like someone fucking and his prick spat cum on his waistcoat. The dwarf was emitting a death rattle convulsing from head to foot.

M A R I E   P I S S E S
O N   T H E   C O U N T

M A R I E kept pissing.

On the table amidst the bottles and the glasses, she sprinkled herself with urine with her hands.

She drenched her legs, her ass, her face.

—Look how pretty I am, she said.

Squatting down, with her cunt at the level of the monster's head, she made her lips open horribly.

MARIE SPRINKLES HERSELF
WITH URINE

M A R I E had a bitter smile.

A vision of bad horror . . .

One of her legs slipped: her cunt struck the count in the head.

He lost his balance and fell.

The two of them crashed down screaming, in an incredible din.

M A R I E   F A L L S
O N T O   T H E   M O N S T E R

ON the ground there was a horrible scuffle.

Marie broke loose, bit the dwarf on the dick and he screeched.

Pierrot knocked her to the ground. He spread out her arms
to form a cross: the others held her legs.

Marie wailed:

    —Leave me alone.

Then she fell silent.

By the end she was panting, her eyes closed.

She opened her eyes. Pierrot, red, sweaty was on top of her.

    —Fuck me, she said.

MARIE BITES THE DWARF
ON THE DICK

—F U C K her, Pierrot, said the barkeeper.

They moved excitedly around the victim.

Marie let her head fall back, annoyed by these preparations.

The others laid her out, opened her legs. She was breathing quickly, her breath was burning.

The scene in its slowness evoked the slaughter of a pig, or the burial of a god.

Pierrot had his pants off, the count required that he be naked.

The delicate young man stamped like a bull: the count facilitated the entrance of his cock. The victim quivered and struggled: bodies locked in incredible hatred.

The others watched, their lips dry, stunned by this frenzy. The bodies knotted together by Pierrot's prick rolled on the ground struggling. At the end, arching forward to the breaking point, completely out of breath, the farmboy howled, slobbering all over himself, Marie responded with a death spasm.

MARIE IS POKED
BY PIERROT

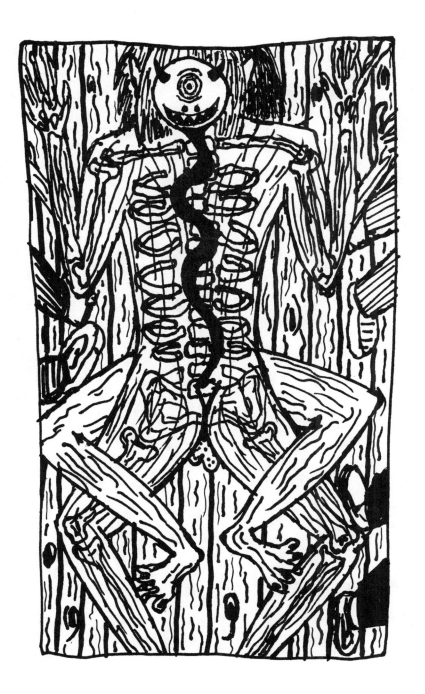

. . . M A R I E came to.

She heard the songs of birds in the branches of a tree.

The songs, of an infinite delicacy, flitted whistling from tree to tree. Stretched out on the moist grass she saw the sky was light: the day was being born at that very moment.

She was cold, seized by a frozen happiness, suspended in an unintelligible emptiness. However much she would have liked to gently lift up her head, and in spite of the fact that she fell back in exhaustion on the ground, she remained faithful to the light, to the foliage, to the birds that peopled the woods. For an instant, occasions of childhood shyness brushed lightly over her, in memory. She recognized, bent over her, the great and massive head of the count.

MARIE LISTENS
TO THE BIRDS
IN THE WOODS

WHAT Marie read in the eyes of the dwarf was the insistence of death . . . this face expressed only an infinite disillusionment, that a frightful obsession made cynical. Hate leapt up in her, and death approaching, she got very frightened.

She raised herself up clinching her teeth in front of the kneeling monster.

Standing, she trembled.

She took a step back, looked at the count and vomited.

—You see, she said.

—Relieved? asked the count.

—No, she said.

She saw the vomit in front of her. Her torn coat barely covered her.

—Where are we going? she said.

—Your place, answered the count.

MARIE VOMITS

—M Y place, groaned Marie. Once again his head turned toward her.

—Are you the devil himself to want to go to my place? she asked.

—Yes, the dwarf came back, they've sometimes told me I was the devil himself.

—The devil? said Marie, I'd shit in the devil's face!

—Just a moment ago you vomited.

—I'd shit.

She squatted down and shit on the vomit.

The monster was still kneeling.

Marie leaned against an oak. She was sweating, in a trance. She said:

—All that, it's just nothing. But *at my place* you'll be scared . . . Too late . . .

She shook her head and, wild, marched roughly up to the dwarf, pulled him by the collar and screamed:

—You coming?

—My pleasure, said the count.

He added, almost quietly:

—She's worth it to me.

MARIE SHITS
ON THE VOMIT

MARIE, who heard him, looked directly at the count. He got up:

—No one, he murmured, ever speaks to me that way.

—You can leave, she said. But if you come . . .

The count interrupted her curtly:

—I follow. You're going to give yourself to me.

She remained violent:

—It's time, she said. Come.

MARIE LEADS OFF
THE COUNT

T H E Y walked swiftly.

Day was breaking when they arrived. Marie pushed on the gate. They took a path lined with old trees: the sun made their heads golden.

Marie in all her surliness knew she was in accord with the sun. She led the count into the room.

—It's over, she said to herself. She was at once weak, full of hatred, indifferent.

—Undress yourself, she said, I'll wait in the next room. The count undressed unhurriedly.

The sun through a clump of leaves speckled the wall and the speckles of light were dancing.

MARIE AND THE GNOME
ENTER THE HOUSE

T H E count got a hard-on.

His dick was long and reddish.

His naked body and his dick had a devilish deformity. His head in his angular shoulders which were raised too far up, was pale and mocking.

He desired Marie and limited his thoughts to his desire.

He pushed open the door. Sadly naked, she waited for him in front of a bed, provocative and ugly: drunkenness and fatigue had beaten her down.

—What's wrong? said Marie.

The dead man, in disorder, filled the room . . .

The count stammered gently.

— . . . I didn't know.

He had to steady himself on a piece of furniture: *he lost his hard-on.*

Marie had a hideous smile.

—*It is accomplished!* she said.

She looked stupid holding out a broken phial in her right hand. Finally, she fell.

MARIE DIES

...FINALLY *the count noticed the two hearses in a row, heading*
slowly toward the cemetery.
The dwarf hissed between his teeth:
  —I was had . . .
He didn't see the canal and let himself slip.
A loud noise, for an instant, disturbed the silence of the water.

The sun remained.

MARIE FOLLOWS
THE DEAD MAN
INTO THE EARTH